Jack's
Big Race

To the memory of Arthur Law,
master mariner, meteorologist, mathematician,
and maker of church organs
who gave us his special wood; and to his wife Kit,
whose grandfather sailed 'The Ebenezer';
and to my son Jack, who built and sailed the raft.

M. F.
St Ives

Jack's Big Race

Written and illustrated by
Michael Foreman

RED FOX

JACK'S favourite place was his grandfather's shed. His family had always been sailors and the shed was an upside-down boat on a beach where the river meets the sea.

It was a small river, but at high tide the sea would rush
upstream and flood the mudflats behind the dunes.

THE shed was full of Grandad's treasures and Jack knew that each and every object had a story.

One morning, Jack pointed at some strange pieces of wood on a rope. They had holes drilled through them in mysterious patterns. "What are these, Grandad? And why are they full of holes?"
"They're from the old church organ," replied Grandad. "The holes are to let the tunes out. My father, your great-grandfather, built the organ. He could do anything – he even built his own boat, *The Ebenezer*, and then he made the organ from the bits left over. He gave me the organ designs and taught me how to mend it too in case it broke."
And he showed Jack how the organ pipes fitted into the holes in the wood.
"Did it ever break, Grandad?"
"I've had to replace a few bits now and again. But I always keep the old pieces. Don't know why. Silly, really."

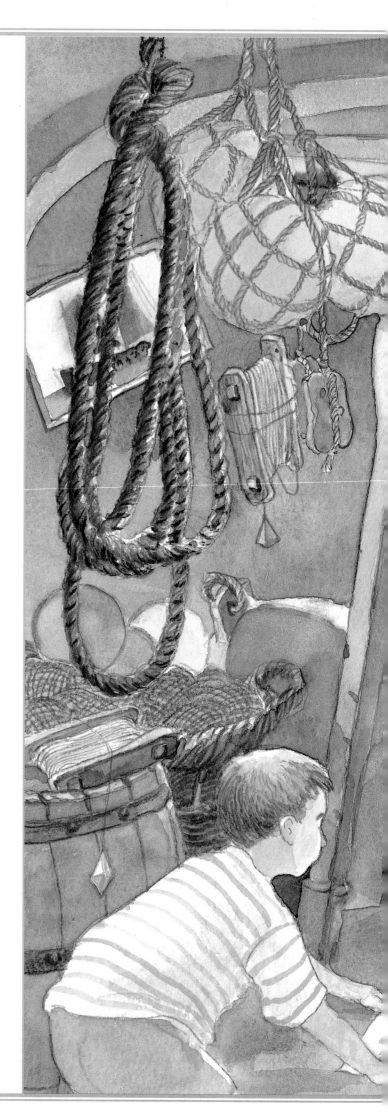

"Is that *The Ebenezer* out there, Grandad?"
"Afraid so, Jack. That's all that's left."
They looked through the porthole at the dark wooden ribs of *The Ebenezer* sticking out of the mud. Cormorants, like vultures, perched on the bones.

"I WANT to be a sailor," said Jack. "Like you and Great-grandfather."

"Well, when you're grown up you can."

"I want to do it now," replied Jack. "I want to build a raft for the raft race this afternoon."

Jack showed Grandad his plan for a raft. He would use part of an old door he had found washed up on the beach. Empty plastic bottles from the cafe would help it float.

"You need outriggers, Jack," said Grandad. "Like they have in the South Seas. To stop it tipping over."

He looked around his shed. "These will do." He took the strange pieces of organ wood and lashed them across the door and tied the plastic bottles on each end.

"But, Grandad, it's your special wood."

"Special wood for a special race," grinned Grandad. "Come on, it will be starting soon."

THEY carried the raft along the shore to the harbour where the race was to take place. It was a scene of wild excitement. There were flags, crowds, and rafts of every description. Jack's raft was by far the smallest.

"Are you sure you want to do this?" asked Grandad.

"It would be a waste of your wood if I didn't," said Jack.

"Don't worry about the old wood," said Grandad. "I've no use for it."

"So why have you kept it all these years?" asked Jack with a grin.

Grandad grinned back. "Take care," he said, "and good luck."

JACK paddled out to the Starting Line. The lifeboat fired a
rocket and the race began. Frantic paddling by the crews
made many of the rafts collide.

Waterbombs and bags of flour flew from raft to raft like an ancient sea battle and some crews were more interested in splashing each other than getting on with the race.

JACK carefully paddled his way through the chaos and emerged from the great cloud of flour in the lead. The crowd went wild. The smallest raft with the youngest paddler was winning!

But there was still a long way to go. When the other crews realised what was happening, they got down to the serious business of catching Jack.

SOME of the big rafts were heavy and slow. Others were overmanned and overturned.

But one, which wasn't really a raft at all, but an inflatable banana, was fast. The crew was from the local rugby club and were the roughest, toughest men in town.

THE winning post was the end of the pier. Jack tried to
keep a regular rhythm but his arms ached and his chest
seemed about to burst.

Then he felt some of the bottles shift under his raft . . .

He saw a rope slip and the raft became unbalanced.
Bottles began bobbing up around him.

Jack kept paddling. He was almost there. But now all the
ropes were slipping . . .

JACK could hear the shouts from the banana crew as they
drew nearer and nearer. He lay flat on the old door and
tried to hold his raft together.

   He gave up all attempts at paddling. He knew it was
hopeless. His race was over.

He remained face down on what was left of his raft, his tears adding salt to the sea. He had lost the race but, worst of all, he had lost Grandad's wood.

The crowd was cheering. Jack could hear the banana crew laughing.

STRONG arms lifted him onto the steps of the pier - and a lady handed him a silver cup. He had won!

The inflatable banana had caught up with him as his raft fell
apart, and had nosed him gently over the Finishing Line –
because the rough, tough, rugby men thought he deserved to win.

THAT evening Jack and Grandad took the silver cup down to the mudflats. "To show *The Ebenezer* there's a new sailor in the family," said Grandad.

But *The Ebenezer* looked different in the moonlight – more flesh on the bones.

Then Jack saw that the wood from his raft, some rope and a bottle or two, were tangled in the ribs of the old boat. They had been carried there by the evening tide.

"Should we get your wood back, Grandad?" asked Jack.

"No. It looks fine there," said Grandad. "It all came from the same tree. It's where it should be."

THEY watched in silence for a while. Then Jack said, "Grandad, could you teach me to mend the old church organ?"

Grandad grinned and put his big sailor's hand round Jack's shoulder. "A chip off the old block," he said. "Just like the wood, you're a chip off the old block."

A<small>ND</small> the wind played tunes through the holes in the wood.

And the Moon danced on the sea.

A Red Fox Book
Published by Random House Children's Books
20 Vauxhall Bridge Road, London SW1V 2SA

A division of The Random House Group Ltd
London Melbourne Sydney Auckland
Johannesburg and agencies throughout the world

1 3 5 7 9 10 8 6 4 2

First published in Great Britain by Andersen Press Ltd 1998

Red Fox edition 2000

Printed in Hong Kong

THE RANDOM HOUSE GROUP Limited Reg. No. 954009
www.randomhouse.co.uk

ISBN 0 09 940495 8